For Tom & Lorna

J C Perry

Published by Four Geckos Publishers.

A catalogue record for this book is available from the British Library.

ISBN: 9781916464339

The Best Nest

A Tale of Roosting Rivalry

Written and illustrated by J. C. Perry

Four Geckos Publishers

In a tree in a field near an old stone wall,

there lived two birds named Peter and Paul.

When they had finished building their nests
Paul looked at Peter's and thought "Whose is best?"

Paul boasted "I've used nice,
warm feathers in mine."

Peter replied "I've used
strong sticks from a vine."

This bothered Paul, so while
Peter was away,
Paul made his nest stronger
with mud and clay.

When Peter got home, Paul boasted "My nest is the best!"
He flapped his wings proudly and puffed out his chest.

Peter felt jealous, so all
through the night,
he worked on his nest
until it was light.

When Paul woke up early,
his beak hit the floor –
there stood a veranda with
a roof made of straw!

Peter sat proudly and
sipped his lemonade.
"Morning Paul" he
tweeted "do you like
what I've made?"

Paul was so furious that
he went **berserk** -

he lifted his toolbag and
set straight to work.

In a flurry of feathers
he transformed his nest,
and when he was
finished there stood a...

...FORTRESS!

It had a drawbridge, turrets and cannons too.
Peter said, "Pah! Is that all you can do?
Mine will be better, and when I'm done,
You'll see that **my** nest is much more fun."

Peter built a
hot tub...

home cinema...

and games room.

And outside
a ferris wheel,
merry-go-round
and log flume!

Paul was dumbfounded, but before he could speak
A flash of lightning silenced his beak.

Rain, then a rumble – a storm was on its way!
The great tree they lived in started to sway.
Peter and Paul lay low in their nests
They'd wait until morning to judge whose was best.

But before morning came, the wind grew stronger.
The nests they'd built could withstand it no longer.

They were too big and heavy – they fell to the ground
in a broken, soggy, twig-tangled mound.

The birds woke the next day near a roaring fire –
A neighbourly owl asked them "Are you feeling drier?"
"What happened to us?" Paul questioned the owl...
"And why do I find myself wrapped in a towel?"

"Your nests were so broken, there was no repair –
You lay in the rain, I couldn't leave you there.
So I picked you both up and I took you with me,
This is where I live, in the trunk of this tree."

She made them a drink

and a quick bite to eat

and they tweeted
some songs while they
warmed up their feet.

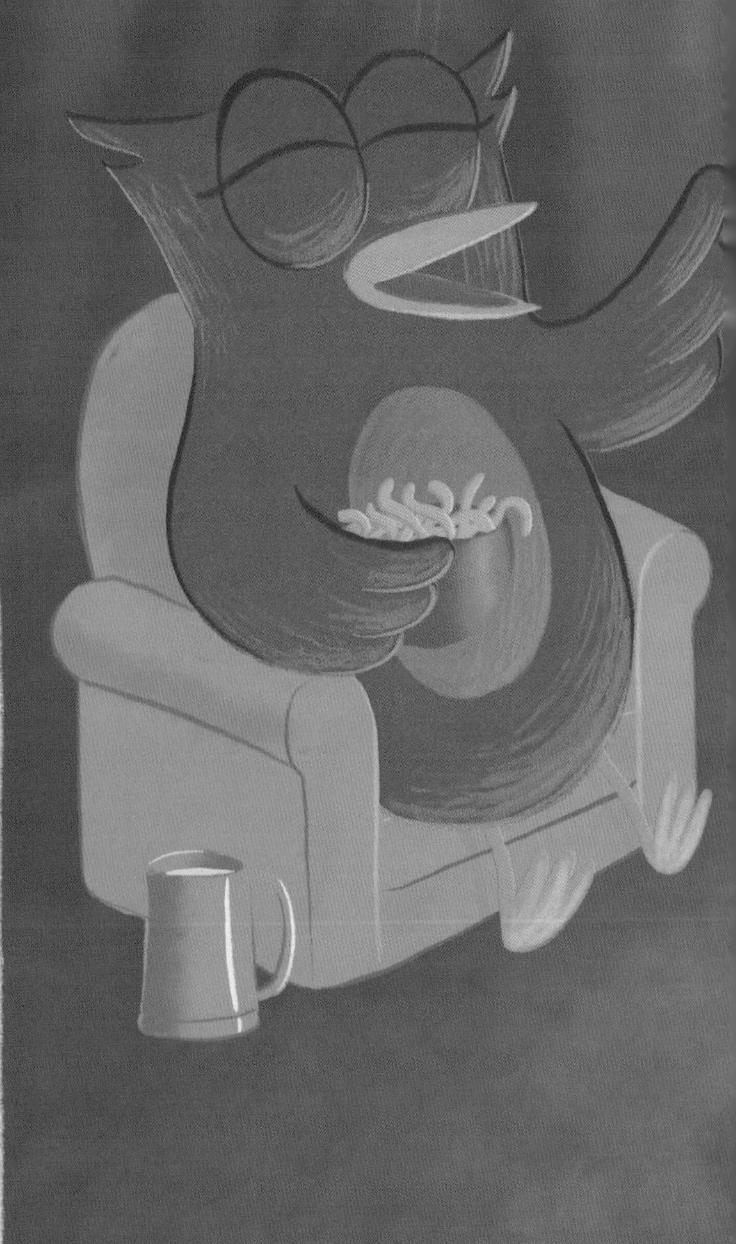

And the owl, thought the birds, didn't have a lot, but this didn't bother the owl, not one jot.

Well this got them thinking, a big fancy nest might not be the true key to real happiness.

A few days went by and in glorious weather
Peter and Paul built a new home **together**.
They had moved to a hole further down the tree
And had painted a 'Welcome' sign for all to see.

Then inside the hollow, they carved rows of beds
And fashioned some blankets out of old threads.

The owl poked her head in as she passed "Why are there so many beds?" she asked.

"You'll find out quite soon," came the answer from Paul and he hung another **WELCOME** sign on the back wall.

Later on that day, the rain started to pour
And wind whipped around their tree once more.

A mole poked
his head out of
his flooded hole

and out of the
wet crawled a
mouse and a vole.

They were joined by others
who'd all lost a home,
they huddled together,
soaked to the bone.

They saw a light glowing through the cold, pouring rain
and found themselves drawn there like moths to a flame.

There stood a tree with a '**Welcome**' sign outside
and two birds who greeted them, wings open wide.
"We're Peter and Paul," the two birds said
"Please help yourself to food and a bed."

The owl was really proud of Peter and Paul.
She cheered "Now you **DO** have the best nest of all!"

THE END

This is me

Hi, I'm J C Perry. I'm a writer, illustrator, animator and graphic designer. My first book 'Wish Upon a Shooting Star' was a finalist in the 2018 Wishing Shelf Book Awards and my second book 'Tom's Zombie Fright' was a silver medal winner in the same awards in 2020. I live and work in Saddleworth with my husband (a fellow animator) and our two kids.

In theory I'm working on my next children's book, although I'm most likely preparing yet another snack for our kids, or hoovering the crumbs up from the last one. After all, you have to keep your nest tidy don't you?

If you enjoyed this book, please leave a review on Amazon or Goodreads. I look forward to reading it.

Other childrens' books I've written and illustrated:

All available to buy in paperback and kindle format from Amazon, or to borrow via Amazon's kindleunlimited

For news about ebook freebies, new books I release and other interesting stuff you might like to know about, please subscribe to the newsletter on my website: www.jcperry.info or follow me on Instagram @j_c_perry

Printed in Great Britain
by Amazon